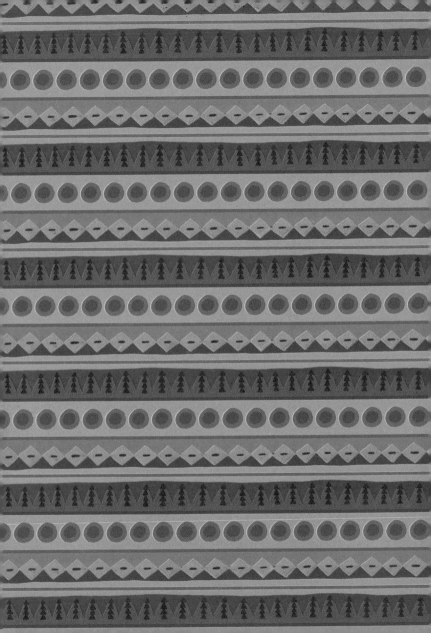

GOOD DOG LION

ALEXANDER McCALL SMITH

GOOD DOG LION

With illustrations by

David Dean

Barrington Stoke

First published in 2014 in Great Britain by
Barrington Stoke Ltd
18 Walker Street, Edinburgh, EH3 7LP

www.barringtonstoke.co.uk

A CIP catalogue record for this book is available
from the British Library upon request

ISBN: 978-1-78112-372-0

*To Edie, Amaya, Maeva
and James Mountain Copping*

Contents

Chapter 1
Sweet Work

This is the story of a boy who lived in Africa. His name was Timo, and he was about 9 years old. I say about 9 years old because nobody, not even his mother, could remember exactly when he was born. That did not matter to Timo or to anybody else – it was good enough for him to be about 9 years old.

Timo lived with his mother. His father had gone off to work somewhere else when Timo was only 4 (or about 4) and he had never come back.

"Perhaps we shall hear from him one day," Timo's mother sighed. "But then, perhaps we shall not."

Timo and his mother lived in a very small house on the edge of a village. Their house had two rooms – a kitchen and a room for sleeping. There was also a sort of bathroom at the back of the house, but it was a bit dark and rather uncomfortable. There was no light in it, so when you went there at night you had to have a torch or candle with you.

The kitchen had a small stove and a shelf for food. There was also a table where Timo's mother did her work. Some of the time she sewed clothes, and some of the time she made jam that she sold at market.

"Sticky work," she said, with a smile.

"Sweet work!" Timo said.

Timo loved his mother's jam, but he was not allowed to put his finger in the pan while she was making it.

But often, when she had finished, she gave him the spoon to lick. Timo loved that – and who wouldn't?

Timo and his mother did not have much money – in fact, they had almost none. But that did not matter too much, because they were happy. Timo had his mother and she had him. They had their little house. They had their jam. They had friends and neighbours. They had the world about them. All of that can be enough for happiness.

Chapter 2
A Wish

In fact, there was one more thing that Timo would have liked to have.

When anybody said to him, what would you ask for if you had one wish, he knew what he would say.

"I'd like a dog."

That could cause surprise. "A dog? Why would you want a dog?" a person would say. "Dogs are a pest. They bark at night and some of them have fleas. They steal food and some of them bite."

"Some," Timo said. "Some dogs do all of those things, but other dogs do not. Some dogs are good dogs. That's the sort of dog I'd like to have."

Timo told his mother about his wish for a dog. "I'd look after it very well, Mother," he promised. "It would be no trouble for you – it really wouldn't."

His mother listened, but shook her head. "I'm sorry, Timo, but we can't have a dog," she said. "You have to feed dogs, you see, and we hardly have enough money for our own food."

"But I'd give him half of mine," said Timo.

"You need your food," Timo's mother said. "You have a lot of growing to do. You can't give half your food to a dog."

Timo was sure he could think of some way round this.

"Then maybe the dog could hunt," he said. "He could go off and find his own food. He could catch rabbits."

"But what if the dog didn't catch anything?" his mother said. "He would be hungry, wouldn't he? And then he might go off and steal food from our neighbours, and what would they think of that?"

Timo knew that his mother might be right. He wished that they had a bit more money and could buy food for a dog, but he did not see how they could get any more. His mother worked hard enough as it was, and he could not see how she could work any harder, even if he helped her more.

Chapter 3
Plum Trees

The help that Timo gave to his mother was to pick the fruit that she used to make her jam. This fruit was not the sort of fruit that farmers grew, but wild fruit that grew on trees in the bush. And sometimes, if he was lucky, Timo also found the hives of wild bees and was able to get honey as well. His mother could sell that for a very good price, and when he found it he knew that she would be very pleased.

Timo picked fruit from a type of wild plum tree. He would climb up the trunk of those trees and then make his way carefully along one of the branches to get to the fruit. Then he would pick it and tuck it into a special bag that his mother had made him for this task.

It was not so easy to harvest the honey. As everybody knows, bees sting when they are angry, and if you try to take their honey, they can get very angry indeed. So what you have to do is to blow smoke into their hive. That stops them from stinging

you and then you can take out some of the honeycomb. You should not take it all, of course, as the bees need some of it themselves, but you can take a large share.

Timo did not always pick fruit by himself. He had a good friend who lived a short way down the road, and this friend would often come with him on these trips to the bush. The boy was called Babu, and he and Timo had been friends since they were very young. They shared everything, and Timo would have done anything for his friend, and his friend would have done anything for him.

The best sort of day was when Timo came back with a big honeycomb and a bag full of fruit.

This would make his mother happy, and she would always give him a slice of the cake that she kept in a tin on the food shelf. This cake was Timo's reward and her way of saying thank you to her son.

"I don't know what I'd do without you," she said. "You're a very good son, Timo."

Timo smiled, but he did not think that he was very good. He thought he was only doing his duty.

"One day, Mother," he said, "I shall be able to look after you and then you won't have to work so hard. I promise you that."

His mother smiled. She knew that Timo meant it, but she also knew that we don't always get what we wish for. But we can still hope for something. There is no rule that says we can't hope. Even if there were such a rule, it was not one that Timo would choose to obey.

Chapter 4
Wild

Then the day came when everything changed.

It was a Saturday, and Timo did not have to go to school. But that did not mean that he could go off and play football, as other boys liked to do – he had to help his mother find fruit for her jam.

He did this cheerfully and without complaint. But he did not go by himself – he asked Babu to come with him. Babu said that he would. He never refused a request from his friend.

Timo had found a very good place for fruit. The only problem with this place was that it was a long walk from their village. It was also in rather wild country, where there were no real paths across the bush.

It was not a place that anybody ever visited, as there were many small hills and wild animals lived in these hills – leopards and baboons. These animals usually kept well away from people, but you would not want to get too close to them. Baboons have long fangs that they will not hesitate to use, and of course leopards have claws. These claws can do a lot of damage to anybody who gets too close to these large spotted cats.

Timo had seen plenty of baboons, but had never seen a leopard. He had heard them sometimes, as they made a coughing sound, rather like somebody clearing his throat. This sound would echo around the rocks and make anybody who heard it feel very uncomfortable.

Timo would have preferred not to pick fruit in that place, but he had picked almost all of the fruit in the nearer parts of the bush. This meant that he had to go further into the bush if he was to get enough fruit for his mother's next batch of jam.

That day the two boys set off, hoping to get back home well before the sun began to sink in the early evening. It was a long walk, and Timo took along a couple of chunks of bread and a bottle of water for their lunch. It was not much of a meal, but it was all they had in the house at the time.

Chapter 5
Top of the Sky

The first part of Timo and Babu's journey was easy, as it took them through fields in which people had planted crops. They saw men and women working in these fields, and waved to them, but as the day wore on they saw fewer and fewer people. And then they saw nobody, as the bush became wilder and wilder and thicker and thicker.

The boys reached the fruit place just as the sun touched the very top of the sky. That was noon, and now the sun would begin its slow journey down towards night. They did not have a lot of time.

Timo and Babu soon found a tree on which lots of ripe fruit was hanging. From that tree alone they would be able to pick enough for Timo's mother to make at least 20 jars of jam. And 20 jars of jam would fetch a good price at the market – Timo's mother could buy enough flour to last them a month.

"You go first," Babu said, and he helped
Timo to climb onto one of the low branches
of the tree.

Once Timo was safely up on the branch, he reached down to pull Babu up too. Then they climbed higher, until they were high enough to pick the fruit.

When their bag was full to the brim, the two boys climbed down the tree, dusted off their clothes, and sat down for their lunch. It had been hard work and they were both hungry, but they could not sit there for long if they were to get home before darkness fell.

Timo looked up at the sun. "We must go now," he said. "We have a long walk back."

Chapter 6
Snake

The two boys started off on their journey.
An hour or so later, although they were
still far from any roads or paths, they
were at least getting out of the thickest
part of the bush. And that was when Timo
reached out and grabbed Babu's arm.

"Did you hear something?" he asked.

Babu shook his head. "I don't think so," he said. "Did you?"

"I think I heard the sound of an animal," said Timo. "But I'm not sure. Let's listen."

They stood very still. The African bush is full of sounds. There are insects that whirr and shriek. There are birds that cry and chatter. There are things that you cannot see that make sounds you can hardly hear. So it is sometimes rather hard to make out just what each sound is.

"There!" Timo said. "There it is again."

This time Babu heard it as well. He looked nervous now. "Do you think it's a leopard?" he asked.

Timo shook his head. "It's not a leopard," he said. "That sound is more like a whimper. I think it's some poor animal in pain."

The sound was coming from somewhere close by. The two boys began to creep towards it. They made sure that they checked where they placed each footstep. There were things down in the grass that could give you a bad bite or sting if you were not careful.

Then they saw him. He was lying in a clump of grass. A dog, with something very wrong with him.

Timo went forward first, while Babu hung back – just in case. But the dog paid no heed to them. His eyes were closed and his breathing was noisy. Every so often he gave a little groan – the sound he had been making when they first heard him.

Timo bent down to examine the dog. He saw that one of his paws was very swollen. He also saw two bright drops of blood in the middle of the swelling. These came from two tiny holes punched in the dog's skin.

"He's been bitten by a snake," Timo called out to Babu. "Come and take a look."

Babu crept forward. "Is he dying?" he asked.

Timo reached out to stroke the dog's head. "He's still alive," he said. "I think we should try to save him."

"Should we carry him all the way home?" Babu asked.

"Yes," said Timo. "He's not a very big dog. He won't be too heavy."

As Timo lifted the dog up, he took care in case he should decide to bite him. But the dog was too ill for that and all he could do was open his eyes a little bit. As he did so, he looked up at the boy who was picking him up and he made a small whimpering sound.

Chapter 7
A Very Serious Thing

Timo and Babu started back again. They took turns to carry the dog, but still the walk seemed much longer. At last they reached Timo's house, just as the sun was setting. Timo's mother came out to meet them.

"What on earth have you got there?" she asked.

"A dog. He's been bitten by a snake,"
Timo explained. "We couldn't leave him
out there to die."

Timo's mother sighed. She was a kind woman, and for all she did not want the dog in the house, she knew that you should never turn your back on an animal in pain. "Bring him in then," she said. "I'll fetch an old sack that he can lie on."

They placed the dog on the sack. Timo fetched a bowl and poured some water into it. He offered this to the dog, but the poor animal was too weak to drink.

"I don't think he's going to live," Timo's mother said. "I'm sorry, but a snake bite can be a very serious thing."

Timo looked at Babu. "We'll look after him, won't we, Babu?" he said.

Babu nodded. "We can take it in turns all night. I'll go and tell my parents that I'll be staying here tonight."

And all that night, while one boy slept, the other took his turn with the dog. They stroked his head gently, and sometimes they tried to get a few drops of water into the animal's mouth. The dog was still in pain, for it whimpered all night.

By the time that morning came, both boys were very tired.

"At least we kept him alive till morning," Timo said. "Now that it's light we can get some help for him."

"How?" Babu asked. "I can't think of anything we can do."

But Timo had a plan. And after breakfast, he thought he would try it.

Chapter 8
The Clinic

There was an animal clinic in the village where Timo lived. The main job of this clinic was to look after cows and other farm animals. But the vet who worked there was a very kind man, and if somebody came in with a sick cat or dog he never had the heart to turn them away. He did not ask people to pay, but he helped cats and dogs out of the kindness of his heart.

The vet was a man who did not like to see animals suffer – even if there was no money for medicines.

Timo had heard about this man, but he had never met him. When he woke up that morning and Babu told him that the dog was no better, he decided to take him to the vet.

"He's the only person who can help him now," Timo said. He examined the dog's paw and saw that it was larger than ever before. "The swelling's not going down, is it?"

Babu shook his head. "I think it's worse," he said.

Now, as they lifted the dog, they could tell that it was very painful for him to be moved. Most dogs will growl or nip if you touch them when they are ill, but this dog did not do that. He just whimpered and closed his eyes in pain.

Timo and Babu took it in turns to carry the dog to the clinic. When they arrived, there was a woman who asked them what they wanted. Timo explained that they had a sick dog.

"The vet's too busy," the woman said in a sharp tone. "You boys can come back tomorrow."

"But our dog could be dead by then," Timo protested.

"Yes," Babu echoed. "He's been bitten by a snake and he's dying. He must see the vet soon."

There was a voice from inside the building. "Did I hear somebody say a dog's been bitten by a snake?"

"They can come back tomorrow," the woman called out. "They must not disturb you."

The vet came out of his office. "No," he said. "Let me look."

Chapter 9
Lion

Timo and Babu held their breath while
the vet bent down to examine the dog. He
prodded at the swollen paw. The dog still
did not growl or try to bite – he seemed to
know that the vet was trying to help him.

The vet shook his head. Timo's heart
sank.

Then the vet spoke. "If you leave him with me, boys," he said, "I'll see what I can do. But ..." He hesitated. "It may be kinder to put him to sleep, you know."

Timo looked up at the vet, pleading with his eyes, but it was Babu who spoke. "Please," he said. "Please don't put him to sleep. He's a good dog, you know."

"I can tell that," the vet said. "He hasn't growled at all."

Timo added his plea. "We'll look after him," he said. "Please try to save his life."

The vet scratched his head. "Well, you know what I'll have to do? I'll have to take off that leg, I'm afraid. There's a very bad infection in it now and the snake's poison has damaged it very badly. I may be able to save his life, but I can't save that leg of his."

"That doesn't matter," Timo blurted out. "As long as he lives, that will be all right."

The vet made up his mind. "Very well," he said. "Come back later and see how he's getting on. I'll keep him here for a few days."

"Thank you," Timo said. He felt a great sense of relief that the dog would live after all.

"By the way," the vet said as he lifted the dog to take him inside. "What's his name?"

Timo thought fast. "Lion," he said.

The vet nodded. "Well," he said, "he's as brave as a lion for sure. It's a good name for him, I think."

The two boys left to go home, but not before they had given Lion a last pat on the head. The dog opened his eyes for a second, and then closed them.

"Goodbye," Timo muttered. "Goodbye, Lion – and good luck."

Chapter 10

Brave

Timo and Babu went back to the clinic later that afternoon. The vet was busy, but the woman they had spoken to in the morning was a bit kinder now. She told them that the operation had gone well.

"The vet thinks your Lion will be all right," she said. "He told me that I could let you see him."

She took them round to the back of the clinic. Lion was lying in a small pen, where there was shade from the sun. His front leg, the one that had been bitten, was now much shorter. It was covered with a large bandage.

"Hello, Lion," Timo whispered. "We can't take you home yet, but we'll come back."

The dog looked at him with heavy eyes.

"He's still very sleepy from the operation," the woman said. "I'll give him

a bit of food before it gets dark. He'll be
hungry, I think."

They left Lion there and started to walk home. They felt sad about what had happened to the dog's leg, but they knew that it was all for the best.

"He'll learn to get by on three legs," Timo said. "Lots of dogs have only three legs."

Babu looked at him. "Do they?" he asked.

Timo shrugged. "I don't know. But I think Lion will be fine."

"Because of his name?" Babu said.

"Maybe," said Timo. "Lots of people live up to their name."

"Do they?" Babu asked.

"Maybe," said Timo. But then he became surer. "Yes, they do. Lion will be every bit as brave as a real lion – in fact, even more."

Chapter 11
Wobbly

Two days later, the boys were able to collect Lion from the clinic. He could not walk home, of course, and again they took turns at carrying him. He still had his bandage, and the vet gave them a spare one and told them how to change it. After that, the vet said, the leg should have healed up.

Timo had spoken to his mother about keeping Lion, but she wasn't keen.

"I know you've always wanted a dog," she said. "But I'm still not at all sure how we're going to feed this Lion of yours."

"A dog with three legs won't need as much food," Timo said.

His mother laughed. "Nonsense! But ..."

Timo pleaded with her. "We can't take him back to the bush."

"No," she said. "We can't ..." And then she gave in. "All right. He can stay."

Timo made Lion a bed out of an old box. He put the bed beside the front door of their house. "He'll look after us," he said.

Lion seemed to be getting better. He did not stand up that day, but the next morning he made his first attempt. He was very wobbly, of course, but he managed. And after that there was his first step. He almost fell down when he tried that, but after a few minutes he seemed to work out how to cope on just three legs.

Soon he was hopping all about their yard, sniffing at this and that, just like a dog with four legs.

"Look at him," Timo's mother said. "He is brave."

Chapter 12
Bones and Scraps

That afternoon, Timo went to the butcher's shop on the edge of the village and spoke to the butcher.

"If you give me some bones and scraps of meat," he said, "I'll tidy your yard for you. I'll also wash your windows."

The butcher thought for a moment. "Every week?" he asked. "You'll do these things every week?"

Timo nodded. "Yes," he said. "I won't let you down. I can work very hard."

"All right," the butcher said. "You can have bones for your dog – and scraps, too. We'll see how it all works out."

It all went very well. Timo was a hard worker, and the butcher was very pleased.

Lion ate the bones and the scrap meat, and he began to put on weight. Now he had a handsome coat and a tail that wagged any time he saw Timo and Babu. They were both very proud of him.

Lion got better at walking too. Even if he could not go very fast, he had worked out how to cope with three legs. He used a sort of hop – he jumped forward with his back legs and then used his single front leg to steady himself before he hopped again. It was a very odd walk, but it did not seem to bother him too much.

Timo and Babu enjoyed teaching Lion tricks, and Lion learned them fast. Soon they had trained him to fetch a ball and bring it back. Then they taught him how to sit when they told him. They thought that Lion was a very clever dog.

"It's almost as if he understands what we're saying," Timo said to Babu.

Lion was standing at their feet. He looked up and barked.

"That's his way of saying 'yes'," Babu said.

Lion barked again.

"And 'no'," said Timo.

Chapter 13
Proud Inside

But there were some people who laughed at Lion.

"Can't you afford a whole dog?" one of the boys at school said.

And another one said, "What's the point of having a dog with three legs?"

Timo ignored them. He did not care if other people laughed at Lion's odd walk. He was proud of his dog because he knew how brave Lion was and how loyal. That was all that mattered.

Timo's mother also became proud of Lion. One day, when she was by herself, a thief came to the house, hoping to steal what little they had inside. Timo's mother was busy with her jam and did not notice the man looking in the window, but Lion did. At first he growled softly, and then, when the man made his way towards the front door, he got to his feet and barked loudly.

The thief could not see that the dog who was making all this fuss only had three legs and he was scared by the noise.

He turned on his heels and fled, followed by Lion. It was a very funny sight, and several people in the village saw it. There was the thief, running for all his worth, with Lion hopping behind him, barking at the top of his voice.

When Timo came home from school and heard about what had happened, he laughed, but he felt very proud inside. That evening he worked extra hard at the butcher's shop and the butcher gave him a large and juicy bone to take away.

"Here's your reward," Timo said to Lion, as he gave him the bone.

Lion wagged his tail and gave his special bark that Timo was sure meant "thank you". The boy did not know it yet, but the next person to say "thank you" would be him. And the "thank you" he would say was going to be a very big one indeed.

Chapter 14
Fetch Help!

This is what happened. Timo's mother had got a large order for jam – about 30 jars. She would be well paid for this, and she was keen to make the best jam possible.

"I know it's a long way away," she said to her son. "But do you think that you and Babu could go to that place where you picked all that good fruit?"

Timo asked Babu whether he could go with him, but Babu had to help his father that day and he could not come.

"I won't be alone," Timo said to his mother. "Lion can come with me."

"But can he walk that far?" his mother asked.

Timo thought that he could and told his mother not to worry. "It might take a little longer," he said. "But we can leave a bit earlier."

It was a hot day, and Timo was pleased that he had brought a large bottle of water with him. Lion was also thirsty and he lapped up the water that Timo offered him in his cupped hands.

As Timo and Lion walked past people in their fields, everybody looked up and stared at the unusual sight. But nobody laughed at Lion's hopping.

"That's a good dog you've got there," one man called out. "I can see he's a plucky dog."

Timo was pleased with the praise and waved at the man. Lion seemed very happy and sniffed the air with interest.

They stopped from time to time, and this gave Lion a chance to rest his back legs, which were tired from all that hopping.

At last, after several stops, they reached the remote and lonely valley where the best fruit trees were to be found. Timo picked a tree with a lot of fruit on the high branches. The wild plums looked plump and juicy. They would be perfect for his mother's jam.

Lion waited at the bottom of the tree while Timo climbed up. And he was there, on the ground below, when Timo crashed out of the tree with a shout.

Timo was not sure why he slipped. Perhaps a branch gave way, or perhaps he lost his grip. Whatever happened, he fell – and he landed with a thud.

It took a moment or two for Timo to discover that he had twisted his right ankle in the fall. When he tried to stand up, a sharp shock of pain ran up his leg and he called out in agony. Lion nuzzled at him, as if to ask him if he was all right.

"I can't walk," Timo said to Lion. "You will have to go for help."

Lion wagged his tail.

"You have to go, Lion," Timo said again. He pointed back down the valley. "That way, Lion! Fetch help!"

The dog hesitated, and then he started to hop off the way Timo was pointing. "That's right, Lion," Timo called out. "That's the way."

Timo soon lost sight of the hopping dog.
He lay back on the ground and tried not
to think of his painful leg. He wondered
how long Lion would take to reach help.
Perhaps he would go to that man who had
been working in the fields. But would the
man understand what Lion was trying to
tell him?

The hours dragged past slowly – as
they always do when you are waiting for
something very important. Timo was
beginning to think that Lion had got lost,

or had decided to chase after a rabbit or something of that sort. 'It could be days before they find me,' he thought. 'And there are snakes about – and leopards.'

But then he heard it. It was a long way away to begin with, then it became louder. It was the sound of a dog barking.

Chapter 15
Lion Jam

Two men came to rescue Timo – the man who had been working in the field, and his friend. Together they carried the boy back to the village, with Lion hopping along behind them.

"That dog has saved your life," one of the men said.

And that is what Timo's mother said too when she brought her son back from the clinic. The doctor said that his ankle was badly twisted, but not broken, and it would get better soon. In the meantime, Timo would have to get about by hopping – just like Lion.

That night, Timo's mother made Lion a special stew, with some of the family's own food, to reward the dog. And as a thank you treat, Lion was able to sleep next to Timo that night, and to lick his hand for comfort when he woke up.

When Timo recovered and was able to go out to pick fruit with Babu again, they took Lion with them. On their first trip, they picked a very large bag of plums that they brought back to Timo's mother with pride. She made a special batch of jam and put a new label on the jars.

"Look," she said, and she showed the boys her new label. "I'm calling it Lion Jam."

The new jam was very popular. Everyone wanted a taste of it. This meant that Timo's mother was able to buy her fruit from farmers, and very soon she was able to build a small shed where she could make even more jam. Timo called his mother's shed her factory. Lion guarded it for her. He was a very good guard dog.

Life became better for that small family. Timo was happy because he had a dog and his mother was happy because now they had more to eat, and some new shoes as well.

And Lion was happy too, because dogs are happy most of the time, even if they have only three legs. What counts for them is having a good home and a good master to love – which Lion had.

"He's a good dog," Babu said.

"Yes," Timo said as he patted Lion's head. "He's a very good dog."

Have you read all the Little Gems?

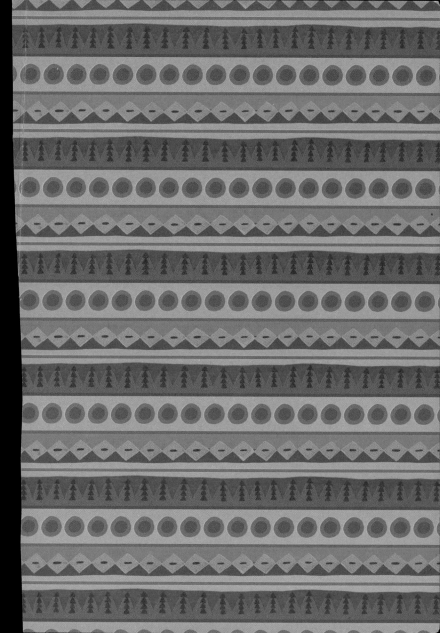

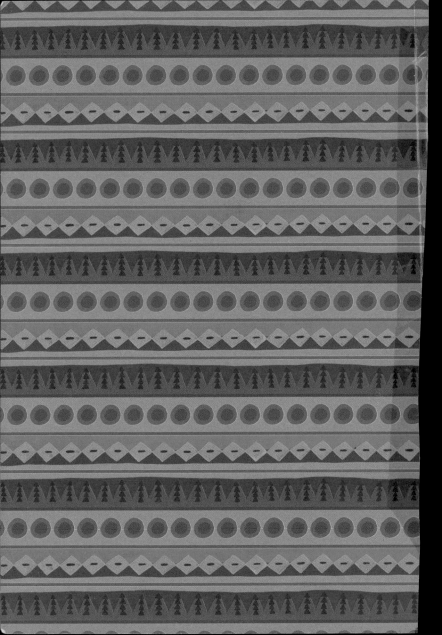

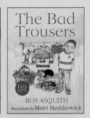